John G. Kotzé

Documents and Correspondence

Relating to the judicial crisis in the South African Republic

John G. Kotzé

Documents and Correspondence
Relating to the judicial crisis in the South African Republic

ISBN/EAN: 9783337382575

Printed in Europe, USA, Canada, Australia, Japan

Cover: Foto ©Andreas Hilbeck / pixelio.de

More available books at **www.hansebooks.com**

DOCUMENTS AND CORRESPONDENCE

RELATING TO

THE JUDICIAL CRISIS

IN THE

SOUTH AFRICAN REPUBLIC

(TRANSVAAL).

TRANSLATED

By J. G. KOTZÉ.

LONDON:

WILLIAM CLOWES AND SONS, LIMITED,

Law Publishers and Booksellers,

27, FLEET STREET.

1898.

NOTE.

I HAVE deemed it advisable to translate and publish the documents and correspondence in my possession, and which were called into existence by the draft measure proposed by President Kruger for the approval of the Transvaal Volksraad. This measure, it will be remembered, was, without any previous publication, hurried through the Volksraad in the short space of three days. By this so-called law, No. 1 of 1897, the President is "empowered to ask the members of the judiciary whether they deem it in accordance with their oath and duty to dispense justice according to the existing and future laws and Volksraad resolutions, and not to *arrogate* to themselves the so-called testing right; and His Honour is further empowered to dismiss from office those members from whom His Honour receives a negative answer, or, in his opinion, insufficient answer, or no answer whatever, within the time given by him for that purpose."

I publish these documents without any comment, as I may probably, at a later date, write fully on the constitutional question, and on the circumstances which have brought about the judicial crisis in the Transvaal. The documents A, B, and C, placed in the Appendix, although not sent to the President, may help to throw light on the subject. The papers B and C will clearly show that both Judges Jorissen and Morice, who have retained their seats on the Bench, agreed with me, in June, 1897, that President Kruger had not merely departed from his undertaking with the judges, but also that the draft-grondwet had to be submitted by the President to the Volksraad in the session of 1897, and not in the session of 1898, as erroneously stated in the *ex post facto* notes of Sir Henry de Villiers.

J. G. K.

DOCUMENTS AND CORRESPONDENCE.

High Court of the South African Republic, Pretoria,
February 23, 1897.

The members of the High Court, in council assembled, resolve, with regard to the draft law which has just been laid upon the table of the Volksraad, as follows :—

1st. To acquaint the State President and members of the Executive in writing of the fact that the said draft law violates the independence of the High Court, and to express the readiness of the Judges amicably and patriotically to co-operate in removing any difficulty, the existence of which is inferred by the Judges from the fact of the proposed law aforesaid.

2nd. In the event of the proposed law being adopted, the High Court and Circuit Court shall be adjourned *sine die*, and due written notice thereof shall be given to the State President and Executive Council, at the same time informing them that the members of the High Court will, by means of a declaration fully setting forth the grounds of their action, appeal to the people.

3rd. In the event of the debate on the proposed law in the First Volksraad being conducted in an improper manner towards the Judges, without any protest from the Chairman, the sittings of the High Court and Circuit Court shall be temporarily suspended.

4th. The members of the High Court bind themselves to stand together in every respect and in every event, and to act together in everything which may directly or indirectly affect any of their number by virtue of the said law. Any interference with any member of the High Court under the said law shall be considered by the members of the High Court as an attack upon the whole body, and joint action shall accordingly be taken thereon.

J. G. KOTZÉ.

H. A. AMESHOFF.

E. J. P. JORISSEN.

GEORGE T. MORICE.

R. GREGOROWSKI.

No. 2.

High Court, Pretoria, February 23, 1897.

The Honourable Dr. W. J. Leyds,
        State Secretary.

HONOURABLE SIR,

I am instructed by the Honourable the Chief Justice and other the Judges of the High Court to request you to bring the accompanying Declaration to the knowledge of His Honour the State President and Executive Council, and through that body to the knowledge of the Honourable the First Volksraad.

I have the honour to be
Your obedient servant,
J. C. JUTA,
Registrar.

No. 3.

High Court, Pretoria, February 23, 1897.

DECLARATION.

The Members of the High Court of the South African Republic have taken notice of the draft law now laid upon the table of the First Volksraad. In all earnestness they desire to inform His Honour the State President and the Executive Council that, in their unanimous opinion, this proposed measure infringes on the independence of the High Court.

The Judges do not take upon themselves to state whether it was desirable to place this law on the table—in that matter they cannot judge. But the love which they have for the land and people forces them to desire His Honour the State President and the Executive Council, and through them the First Volksraad, to postpone the consideration of this draft law till the usual sitting in May, with a view to letting the voice of the people be heard. In their opinion the matter can be postponed, and at the present moment there is no danger of legal uncertainty, which, however, may occur through the over-hasty acceptance of the draft measure now on the table.

Should the Honourable the First Volksraad decide to elect a Committee from its midst to consider the difficulties of this question and to remove them, the Judges hereby offer their assistance, in the conviction that a satisfactory and friendly solution will be arrived at.

J. G. Kotzé.

H. A. Ameshoff.

E. J. P. Jorissen.

George T. Morice.

R. Gregorowski.

No. 4.

High Court, February 24, 1897.

The State Secretary.

Sir,

After an interview with my colleagues, and invited thereto by the Executive Council, I have, as Chief Justice, upon request of my colleagues, drawn up a draft. Upon discussing this draft, the Judges desired time to consider the matter, and it is for this reason that I am unable for the moment to furnish you with a draft. The subject is of too weighty a nature to be hurriedly dealt with.

I have the honour to be, Sir,

Your obedient servant,

J. G. Kotzé,

Chief Justice.

No. 5.

Government Office, February 24, 1897, 2 p.m.

His Honour
The Chief Justice.

HONOURABLE SIR,

With reference to your communication of even date just now received, in which you state that you are not able to send in an immediate draft, I am instructed by the State President to request you to send in during the course of the day the points in the draft law now under discussion against which the Judges take exception.

I have the honour to be

Your obedient servant,

Dr. W. J. Leyds,

State Secretary.

No. 6.

Pretoria, February 24, 1897.

The Honourable Dr. W. J. Leyds,
State Secretary.

SIR,

Your letter of this afternoon has reached me. I will call my colleagues together, and, after having seen them, I will, as soon as possible, send you an answer.

Your obedient servant,

J. G. Kotzé,

Chief Justice.

No. 7.

Government Office, Pretoria, February 24, 1897.

The Honourable J. G. Kotzé,
Chief Justice, Pretoria.

YOUR HONOUR,

I have the honour to inform you that it is not impossible that the Executive Council, which meets to-morrow morning at eight o'clock, will wish to see you and your colleagues soon after, in which event I will let you know. I have apprised you of this, seeing that the members of the Executive will have to be present in the Volksraad as soon as it resumes its sitting, and the time at their disposal is limited.

I have the honour to be
Your obedient servant,
DR. W. J. LEYDS,
State Secretary.

No. 8.

High Court, February 25, 1897, 10 a.m.

MEMORANDUM.

This morning the Judges were, upon request, present in the Executive Council. Besides the undersigned, there were present the State President, the Vice-President, State Secretary, Mr. J. M. A. Wolmerans, Mr. J. Kock, Mr. P. Cronjé, and the State Attorney.

The State President intimated to the Judges that he had expected from them *a written statement of their objections against the proposed law* now upon the table of the First Volksraad, and under discussion.

The Chief Justice hereupon observed that " only four Judges were present, as Mr. Justice Morice had left for Johannesburg in order to continue the adjourned sitting of the Circuit Court for Criminal cases. The Judges had on the previous day held a long consultation, after their presence in the Executive

Council, and the point for consideration was the submission of *a solution out of the difficulty which existed.* After that a letter addressed to the Chief Justice was in the afternoon received by him from the State Secretary, asking that the Judges *would set forth their objections to the proposed law.* While the Judges were considering this letter, a further written communication was received from the State Secretary, intimating that there was a possibility that the Judges would again be invited to attend the Executive Council. The gravity of the matter manifested itself the moment the Judges, in consultation assembled, began to discuss the same. The State President now says that we have not handed in *our objections.* It may now be briefly observed that the Judges are entirely opposed to the principle as well as to the proposed law in its entirety. Both are grave violations of the independence of the Judiciary. The Judges are prepared to suggest a solution, after having first calmly and seriously considered the question, for they can not and dare not act hurriedly and inconsiderately in so important a matter. This is their unanimous opinion. With a deep sense of their duty and of the gravity of the moment, the Judges advise the postponement of the proposed law until the voice of the people shall have been heard, or the withdrawal of the proposed law altogether."

J. G. KOTZÉ.
H. A. AMESHOFF.
E. J. P. JORISSEN.
R. GREGOROWSKI.

No. 9.

RESOLUTION ADOPTED AT A MEETING OF ADVOCATES AND SOLICITORS, HELD AT JOHANNESBURG THIS 25TH DAY OF FEBRUARY, 1897.

This Meeting, having considered the provisions of the draft law concerning the powers of the Judiciary, is of opinion that the principle of the law is not merely bad, but decidedly dangerous, inasmuch as it serves to deprive the Court of its independence, which forms the principal bulwark of the rights and liberties of the people.

Unanimously adopted.

J. JOHNSON HOYLE.	H. L. LINDSAY.
W. F. LANCE.	WM. NIXON.
D. J. DE VILLIERS.	WM. V. MORKEL.
W. T. H. FROST.	F. M. BLUNDELL.
EDWIN C. TENNANT.	P. CHAS. JACOBSOHN.
W. LINCH.	A. TORN.
C. L. BOTHA.	R. BAUMANN.
A. MORICE.	H. DE V. STEYTLER.
H. J. STONESTREET.	H. J. RAUBENHEIMER.
H. C. HULL.	CHARLES H. MULLINS.
JOHN G. KERR.	HAROLD FRY.
E. MAWLY.	A. B. VAN OS.
H. ROSE-INNES.	JNO. G. AURET.
H. HOFMEYR.	WALTER E. HUDSON.
F. WM. BEYERS.	LOUIS L. PLAYFORD.
NAPH. H. COHEN.	H. W. SMITH.
W. H. DICKENSON.	H. LORENTZ.
W. VAN HULSTEYN.	FRANK C. DUMAT.
ROBT. W. HEARLE.	S. ZWARENSTEIN.

T. VAN EXTER.

No. 10.

High Court of the S.A. Republic, Pretoria, February 26, 1897.

His Honour, the State President,
and Members of the Executive Council.

YOUR HONOUR AND GENTLEMEN,

The undersigned having read the speech delivered yesterday in the Honourable the First Volksraad by the State Secretary, and the motion which was in consequence thereof adopted, are not in a position to judge whether the report of the said speech as published in the newspapers is correct. In case the published report is correct, they can only express their regret at what has occurred, for the Judges never at any time

stated that they were not able to submit a solution or remedy of
the supposed difficulty. All that the Judges have done was
merely to point to the very short time allowed them, and to the
fact that the original request of the Government was almost
immediately replaced by another, on account of which a misunderstanding seems to have arisen.

> We have the honour to be
> Your obedient servants,
> > J. G. KOTZÉ.
> > H. A. AMESHOFF.
> > E. J. P. JORISSEN.
> > GEORGE T. MORICE.
> > R. GREGOROWSKI.

No. 11.

Government Office, Pretoria, February 26, 1897.

The Honourable the Chief Justice
and Puisne Judges of the High Court, Pretoria.

YOUR HONOURS,

In reply to your communication of to-day's date,
I have the honour, on behalf of His Honour the State President
and Members of the Executive, to inform you that if the report
of my words, as stated by you, has been published in the newspapers, such report is inaccurate. The Members of the Executive
think it advisable that the Official Minutes should be consulted,
which will furnish you with a different reading.

> I have the honour to be
> Your obedient servant,
> > DR. W. J. LEYDS,
> > State Secretary.

No. 12.

The Judges of the High Court have taken notice of the fact,
that the draft law, introduced by the State President during
the past week into the Honourable the First Volksraad in its
special session, has been approved by that body. They feel

deeply grieved that thereby a vital violation of the independence of the judiciary has taken place. It is among others proposed and passed that the Judges, who hold their appointment for life, and who can only be dismissed for official misconduct, after a proper trial, shall be deprived of these safeguards to the imminent danger of the liberty and property of the citizens. The Judges are, moreover, in consequence of what has been done, exposed in future to the suspicion of bribery, and the power is also given to the State President, to privately and extrajudicially interpellate the Judges, on pain of their dismissal, whereas they ought only to express their opinions officially from the Judgment seat after proper argument and discussion in open Court.

The Judges as such are servants of the people, and fear that, through the hasty action which has been taken, results imperilling the liberty of the Republic may be brought about. Their patriotism, therefore, dictates that in such a state of tension they should quietly, and as long as possible, continue to administer justice. They, however, regret that the proposed new scheme of sitting from day to day can at present not be carried out. The term will, therefore, as usual, close with the fifth day of March. They calmly and quietly await the decision of the people, who have entrusted the administration of justice into their hands, on what has happened. Every one must submit to the clearly expressed and considered will of the people. Loyalty to the State and respect for the people induce them to adopt this course.

J. G. KOTZÉ.

H. A. AMESHOFF.

E. J. P. JORISSEN.

GEORGE T. MORICE.

R. GREGOROWSKI.

Resolved to read this Declaration openly from the Bench on Monday morning, 1st March, 1897.

J. G. KOTZÉ.

H. A. AMESHOFF.

E. J. P. JORISSEN.

GEORGE T. MORICE.

R. GREGOROWSKI.

No. 13.

Government Office, Pretoria, March 4, 1897.

The Honourable J. G. Kotzé,
    Chief Justice of the S.A. Republic, Pretoria.

YOUR HONOUR,

    I am instructed by His Honour the State President to ask you, in consequence of Article 4 of Law No. 1, 1897, whether you consider it in accordance with your oath and duty to administer justice according to the existing and future laws and Volksraad resolutions, and not to arrogate to yourself the so-called testing right.

His Honour expects your answer on or before Wednesday, the 17th March next.

    I have the honour to be
        Your obedient servant,
            DR. W. J. LEYDS.

No. 14.

High Court, March 5, 1897.

The members of the High Court of the South African Republic have received notice from three of their number, viz. the Chief Justice, J. G. Kotzé, H. A. Ameshoff, and E. J. P. Jorissen, that letters have been addressed to them in which a certain question is put to them by the State Secretary on behalf of the State President. The Judges, regard being had to the authority to which the State President appeals enabling him to have the question put, observe that the State President is authorised by the Volksraad to put the question to the present members of the Judiciary, while no authority is given to question only certain individual members of the Court. The Judges are of opinion that the three members above named can give no answer until the question has been put to all the present members of the Bench. They, however, seriously and earnestly advise the withdrawal of the letters, in the interests of the rights of the sovereign people. If this be not done, the holding of the Circuit Courts, which commence on Monday next and continue till about the end of May, will suffer serious obstruction, while, moreover, irreparable legal uncertainty may be occasioned thereby. The Judges accordingly trust that they may receive an answer to this communication before noon to-morrow (Saturday), 6th March.

J. G. KOTZÉ.
H. A. AMESHOFF.
E. J. P. JORISSEN.
GEORGE T. MORICE.
R. GREGOROWSKI.

No. 15.

High Court of the S.A. Republic, Pretoria, March 5, 1897.

In the written announcement made by the Chief Justice, on behalf of all the Judges, on Monday last, it was stated that they had resolved to continue the administration of Justice as long as possible. Letters addressed yesterday, on behalf of the President to three of the Judges, frustrate the intention of the Judges for the present in that respect, and they have resolved to adjourn the High Court and the sittings *in camera* until Monday, the 8th March.

J. G. KOTZÉ.
H. A. AMESHOFF.
E. J. P. JORISSEN.
GEORGE T. MORICE.
R. GREGOROWSKI.

No. 16.

Government Office, Pretoria, March 6, 1897.

YOUR HONOURS,

I have the honour to acknowledge the receipt of a resolution of the Judges, a copy of which was forwarded to me by the Registrar under cover of 5th March. I have communicated the same to His Honour the State President. His Honour instructs me to inform you that His Honour cannot agree with your interpretation of the authority conferred upon him by the Volksraad, and that His Honour cannot withdraw the letters addressed to Chief Justice Kotzé and the puisne Judges Ameshoff and Jorissen.

His Honour desires me to further inform you that he has no reason for putting the question mentioned in Art. 4 of Law No. 1, 1897, to the puisne Judges Morice and Gregorowski, inasmuch as it has not appeared to His Honour that these two Judges question the validity of laws and Volksraad resolutions.

As, however, His Honour infers from the resolution aforesaid that it is the desire of these two Judges to receive a letter similar to that already sent to the others, I have received instruction to comply with such desire, which will be done during the day.

In conclusion, His Honour trusts that the holding of the Circuit Courts will not be interrupted, as, in his opinion, no reason therefor exists.

I have the honour to be

Your obedient servant,

Dr. W. J. Leyds,

State Secretary.

No. 17.

High Court, Pretoria, March 8, 1897.

The Chief Justice and other Judges of the High Court acknowledge the receipt of the communication of 6th March, 1897, forwarded to them by the State Secretary on behalf of the State President, and received late on the afternoon of Saturday. The Judges have taken notice of the intimation that the State President cannot withdraw the letters addressed last Thursday to the Chief Justice, and Judges Ameshoff and Jorissen. They have also taken notice of the remark that it is the desire of Judges Morice and Gregorowski also to receive a letter similar in terms to that addressed to the other Judges. The Judges think that, as this point is more a matter of a personal nature, it can be personally dealt with by the two Judges concerned.

The expression of trust, however, conveyed by the State President at the end of his letter, compels the intimation that the Judges are unable at present to hold any Circuit Court, seeing that the letters in question have not been withdrawn. It will, therefore, be necessary for the State President to appoint an acting Judge to preside at the Circuit Court sittings, which have now commenced. For this purpose the sitting of the Circuit Court at Heidelberg stands adjourned until ten o'clock to-morrow, Tuesday morning, 9th March. The Judges will require all the time between to-day and the seventeenth for the purpose of finishing arrear judgments.

J. G. KOTZÉ.
H. A. AMESHOFF.
E. J. P. JORISSEN.
GEORGE T. MORICE.
R. GREGOROWSKI.

No. 18.

Government Office, Pretoria, March 8, 1897.

The Honourable J. G. Kotzé,
    Chief Justice, Pretoria.

YOUR HONOUR, .
        I have the honour herewith to inform you that the Government has been pleased to appoint Dr. Johannes Esser provisionally as acting puisne Judge of the High Court of the Republic.

Dr. Esser has this day taken the requisite oath before His Honour the State President, and the members of the Honourable the Executive Council.

I have the honour to be
        Your obedient servant,
            DR. W. J. LEYDS,
                State Secretary.

B

No. 19.

Pretoria Club, Pretoria, March 16, 1897.

MY DEAR CHIEF JUSTICE,

       The following undertaking is what I had in my mind when I wrote my last.

" The Judges, after careful consideration of His Honour the President's letter, have come to the conclusion that, under the special and critical circumstances in which the country is placed, it becomes their duty to answer the questions put to them. They wish it to be clearly understood that their doing so is to form no precedent for the future. Their answer is that Law No. 1 of 1897, whatever opinion they may entertain as to its principle, now forms part of the laws of the land, and that consequently, so long as they remain Judges of the land they must abide by present and future laws and Volksraad besluiten, and not exercise the power of testing whether such laws and besluiten are in accordance with the Grondwet."

      *   *   *   *   *

Believe me, yours sincerely,

J. H. DE VILLIERS.

No. 20.

Pretoria, Wednesday, March 17.

DEAR SIR HENRY DE VILLIERS,

       At a meeting of the Judges last night your suggestion of the answer the Judges should give to the question put them by the President on the new measure, which has recently been sanctioned by the Volksraad, was duly considered. We, however, unanimously came to the conclusion that under the existing circumstances an answer of the nature proposed by you could not be subscribed to by us.

Believe me, yours very sincerely,

J. G. KOTZÉ.

No. 21.

High Court of the S.A. Republic, Pretoria, 17, 3, 1897.

The Honourable Dr. W. J. Leyds,
      State Secretary.

SIR,
      Owing to the absence of His Honour the State President, I have received instruction from the Chief Justice and other the Judges, to inform you that the Judges have resolved to send in their answer to the question put to them after the return of the State President.

      I have the honour to be
      Your obedient servant,
      J. C. JUTA,
      Registrar.

No. 22.

High Court of the South African Republic, Pretoria, 19, 3, 1897.

His Honour
    The State President.

YOUR HONOUR,
      The Judges have the honour, in reply to the communication addressed to them on your behalf, and in which a certain question is put to them, to answer as follows :—

They deeply regret that the Honourable the Volksraad has authorized your Honour to put a certain question to them, and were it not for the existence of exceptional circumstances, they would not feel at liberty to give any answer. The exceptional circumstances which justify them to depart from a well-recognized principle are : 1st, that the Government and Volksraad have been placed somewhat in a difficult position by a recently pronounced Judgment, however honestly and conscientiously given ; 2nd, that the point at issue affects an important constitutional question which seldom comes up for decision ; 3rd, that under the present circumstances of the country, a conflict between the legislative and judicial powers should, if possible, be avoided.

For these reasons the Judges feel at liberty to give the following answer. Considering that conflicting decisions have been given by the High Court with regard to the exercise of the testing right, and considering that some of the members of the Court are of opinion that it does not possess this right, and especially after the clear opinion of the Honourable the First Volksraad on the point, the Judges will not test existing and future laws and resolutions of the Volksraad by reference to the Grondwet.

The Judges declare this on the understanding that your Honour will, as speedily as possible, submit a draft to the Honourable the Volksraad, whereby the constitution or Grondwet (guaranteeing among others the independence of the High Court) will be placed upon a sure basis, so that no alterations can be made therein than by means of special legislation alone, after the example of the provisions on the subject contained in the Constitution of the Orange Free State. In the drawing up of such a draft the Judges are prepared to give the Government and the Volksraad every assistance.

The Judges have the honour to be
Your obedient servants,
J. G. Kotzé.
H. A. Ameshoff.
E. J. P. Jorissen.
George T. Morice.
R. Gregorowski.

No. 23.

Government Office, Pretoria, March 22, 1897.

The Honourable the Chief Justice
and Puisne Judges of the S.A. Republic, Pretoria.

Your Honours,

I am instructed by His Honour the State President to inform you, in answer to your communication of 19th instant, addressed to His Honour, that he acquiesces therein.

His Honour wishes to add that he believes the Judges, who have decided the case of Brown, have acted honestly according to their conviction and conscience, and that the only reason why His Honour proposed the measures contained in Law No. 1 of 1897 to the Volksraad was because he deemed the safety of the State and the certainty of title in property to have been endangered by the said decision.

It is a matter of satisfaction to His Honour the State President, to notice that the observations of the Judges with regard to the Grondwet agree with the plans and intentions which His Honour had already formed on the subject. His Honour at the same time conveys his thanks to the Judges for their statement that they are prepared to render the Government and Volksraad every possible assistance in connection therewith.

I have the honour to be

Your obedient servant,

Dr. W. J. Leyds,

State Secretary.

No 24.

Pretoria, March 23, 1897.

To Advocate Auret and other Members of the Bar, and to Attorney H. J. Hofmeyr and other members of the Side-bar, Johannesburg.

Gentlemen,

On behalf of the members of the High Court, it is my pleasant task to give expression to the high appreciation the Judges entertain of your united endeavours to support them. Our joint object is, and remains, once and for all, to obtain a guarantee of the independence of the Judiciary in the discharge of its duties by a constitution which can only be altered by special legislation and in a special manner.

The State President has given the assurance that he will without delay submit a draft with that object to the Honourable the Volksraad. On this understanding the Judges have deemed it their duty to settle the difference that has unfortunately arisen by an amicable arrangement in order to place no obstacle in the way of bringing about the triumph of the truly constitutional and republican principle above referred to. By granting and securing to each Power in the State its just due through the constitution the welfare and safety of the Republic are promoted in the highest measure.

I have the honour to be
Your obedient servant,
J. G. Kotzé,
Chief Justice.

No. 25.

Pretoria, May 6, 1897.

His Honour S. J. P. Kruger,
    State President.

Your Honour,

Grant me, amid the many matters which at present occupy your time, your kind attention for a single moment. I will be brief. I have noticed with pleasure article 17 of your speech, delivered on Monday last, the 3rd May, on the occasion of the opening of the Honourable the First and Second Volksraad. Regard being had to our mutual object, I must point to the fact that, according to the understanding arrived at between the State President and the Judges, the basis thereof is that the Grondwet shall contain a provision prescribing how alone it can be altered by means of special legislation, after the manner of the Orange Free State Constitution, and that the guarantees for the independence of the Judiciary shall also be incorporated in such Grondwet. Towards the end of the month the ordinary Circuit Court sittings will have terminated, when the Judges will be pleased to give the Government and the Volksraad the necessary assistance.

I sign myself with respect,
Your Honour's
Obediently,
J. G. Kotzé.

No. 26.

Pretoria, May 7, 1897.

DEAR SIR HENRY DE VILLIERS,

In order to simplify matters, I deemed it right to address the enclosed communication to President Kruger. As it was through your mediation that His Honour agreed to accept the basis of the written understanding arrived at between the Head of the State and the Judiciary, the responsibility incurred by you induces me to send you a copy of the letter addressed to the President.

I have mentioned to my colleagues the question of the publication of the correspondence which took place between us during your recent visit to Pretoria, and while they agree with me that there is no necessity for immediate publication, we wish to reserve to ourselves the right of publication should it eventually become necessary to exercise it.

I think of returning to the Cape in a few days' time in order to enjoy the rest of my holiday.

Believe me, with kind regards,

Yours sincerely,

J. G. KOTZÉ.

No. 27.

June 2, 1897.

TELEGRAM.

From Kotzé.　　　　　　　To Sir Henry de Villiers,

Wynberg.

I much regret to inform you that President has departed from solemn promise contained in written understanding come to between His Honour and Judges. Instead of submitting to Volksraad a draft amendment of the constitution, containing a provision analogous to article 26 of Free State Constitution, he has asked Volksraad, which has appointed committee out of its number in consequence, to revise the Grondwet. Such step is likewise contrary to Arts. 13 and 66 of existing Grondwet, 1858.

Action of President unintelligible to me, especially in face of my private letter to him of 6th May, copy of which you possess. President's promise to Judges is promise to you and to civilized world as well. I am reluctantly compelled to summon my colleagues immediately and to consider necessity of proposing withdrawal of Judges' written answer of 19th March. Have not yet received your promised letter.

June 2, 1897, 4.53 p.m.

From Chief,   To Chief Justice Kotzé,
     Cape Town.   Pretoria.

Just leaving. Would it not be well to see what alteration Committee makes. Read my notes of interview.

No. 28.

High Court of the S.A. Republic, Pretoria, July 8, 1897.

His Honour
     The State President.

YOUR HONOUR,

As Chief Justice of the Republic I have taken notice of the official minutes of the Honourable the First Volksraad, as published in the supplement of the Gazette of Wednesday, 9th June, and Wednesday, 16th June, 1897. Therein I find, under the proceedings of Monday, 31st May, 1897, Art. 185, that a Government Missive 796/97, of 19th May, 1897, was placed on the order. This Government communication contains an Executive Council Resolution of 29th April, 1897, which reads as follows :—

"The Executive Council, considering the letter of His Honour the State President to the members of the High Court on the 22nd March, 1897, considering that it is desirable that the Grondwet (Law No. 2, 1896) should be further revised, and that all provisions which do not strictly appertain to a Grondwet should be expunged therefrom, considering that it is desirable to clearly define the province and the independence of the various powers in the State, considering that such a revision of Law No. 2, 1896, will also necessitate a revision of several other laws, and considering further the pressing necessity of systematically arranging the local laws of the Republic, and, wherever necessary, to add to, amend, and explain the same, Resolves to advise His Honour the State President to propose to the Honourable the First Volksraad the appointment of a Commission of three or five members, whose duty it will be, in conjunction with the Government,

(a) "To draft proposals, in consequence of the above considerations, for the revision of the Grondwet (Law No. 2, 1896).

(b) "To add thereto such provisions as will render it impossible to alter the Grondwet, except in the manner provided by the Grondwet itself.

(c) "To compose a whole, or more than one whole, whereby the existing laws of the South African Republic shall be systematically arranged, and where necessary amplified, amended, or more clearly defined.

(d) "To hand in to the Government such revision and all such further proposals and recommendations with regard to this subject as the Commission shall deem fit, with a view to publication in the *Gazette* and confirmation by the Honourable the First Volksraad."

After some discussion the First Volksraad, under Art. 189, took the following resolution :—

"The First Volksraad, regard being had to the Government Missive of 19th May last, B.B. 1221/97, containing an Executive Council resolution, having for its object a revision of the Grondwet, Resolves to approve of the said proposals, and to elect a Commission of five members from its midst, with a mandate to act in conjunction with the Executive Council and the Attorney-General in accordance with the aforesaid proposals, and Resolves further to instruct the Memorial Committee to hand over the petitions (if any) on the subject of a revision of the Grondwet to the said Commission."

Permit me to draw your Honour's attention to the terms of

the letter of the Judges to the State President on 19th March, 1897, and the written reply of your Honour on the 22nd March thereto. From these two documents it clearly appears that the Judges have undertaken not to test laws and resolutions of the Volksraad by reference to the Grondwet under the distinct understanding that you would as speedily as possible submit to the Honourable the Volksraad a *draft measure*, whereby the Constitution or Grondwet (guaranteeing *inter alia* the independence of the High Court) shall be placed upon a sure basis, so that no alterations can be made therein, except by special legislation, in a manner analogous to the provisions on the subject contained in the Constitution of the Orange Free State. The Judges at the same time tendered their services in the framing of such a draft. All this was, without any qualification, agreed to by you.

I feel myself compelled to observe that, in my humble opinion, this understanding has been departed from. No draft measure as aforesaid has, with the aid of the Judges, as they had a right to expect from the letter of the State President of 22nd March, 1897, been submitted by your Honour to the Honourable the Volksraad. The Volksraad has indeed been asked to appoint a Commission in order to regulate several matters in connection with Law No. 2 of 1896. In my view the entrusting to a Volksraad Commission of the task which your Honour, as State President, has taken upon yourself to perform, is not in compliance with the understanding arrived at in March last. It may perhaps be suggested in answer to this that there is nothing to prevent the State President from adopting any proposal by the Volksraad Commission for a revision of the Grondwet as agreed upon in the said understanding as his own, and to submit it to the Volksraad. This answer is, however, open to a twofold objection. In the first place, the State President has undertaken, after having consulted the Judges, to submit a draft measure to the Volksraad, and now he has chosen to adopt another course; and, secondly, the State President has undertaken to do this as speedily as practicable, that is, as speedily as possible. The Commission of the First Volksraad, however, has, so far as a limitation

of time is concerned, received no instructions, nor does any
such limitation appear in the resolution proposed by the
Government and approved by the Volksraad.

As already observed, it has been agreed upon in the understanding that the draft measure shall, as soon as possible, be
submitted to the Volksraad. Under sections *c* and *d* of the
Government proposal, adopted by the Volksraad, it is laid down
that the existing laws shall be collected in one or more systematic whole, and that further proposals and suggestions, as the
Commission may deem necessary, shall be sent in. However
desirable it may be to collect the existing legislation into one
systematic body, such is a gigantic task, which will probably
take a commission of experienced experts more than from two
to three years to complete. Moreover, the understanding
arrived at between the State President and Judges does not
depend upon this point. The Judges have not bound themselves to await the completion of this task.

I wish to observe that the local laws cannot be properly
collected into one harmonious whole, until after the Grondwet
has first been adopted, for all other laws must be shaped in
accordance with its provisions, and no law in conflict with the
Constitution can have or continue to have any validity. The
importance of the subject, and love for true and pure Constitutional and Republican principles, compel us, therefore, to
adhere to the understanding come to between the State
President and the Judges before the eyes of the people and of
the civilized world, and to separate the necessary amendments
with regard to (*a*) the altering of the Grondwet by special
legislation in a manner analogous to the Constitution of the
Free State; and (*b*) the guarantees for the independence of the
Judiciary, from the proposal to collect the local laws into a
systematic whole. The former is emphatically a question of
urgency; the latter, although highly desirable, is not urgent,
and will, from the very nature of the case, take a comparatively
long period of time, which would be contrary to the understanding already mentioned.

It is a simple matter to return to the course indicated in the
understanding. A draft Grondwet already exists. In January,

1894, a Government Commission composed of experienced lawyers submitted a draft constitution to the Government, which at the time received your approval, inasmuch as you caused it to be published in a *Gazette* Extraordinary on the 1st February, 1894. There is nothing to prevent this draft, which, to a very considerable degree, provides for the objections raised by the Judges, from being again laid before the Volksraad ; and I make bold to add that, if this draft had been adopted as a Grondwet, the difficulty and collision which arose in February and March, 1897, could never have occurred. In certain respects this draft will probably need amplification or improvement, in order, *inter alia*, to provide for the needs of the new population of the country. Such can, however, be done without any trouble; and the Judges, I do not for a moment doubt, will afford your Honour every possible assistance therein. I do not wish to obtrude, but merely desire that the Judges shall, in terms of the understanding, be previously consulted.

I have alone approached your Honour on this occasion, and know not whether I am to presume that the other Judges, who together with me signed the letter of 19th March last, must be taken to have departed from the position which they have therein assumed. I may not remain silent when duty compels me to speak. It is my desire that all possible difficulty may be prevented. With me the pure, dignified, and independent administration of justice stands pre-eminent. Does it not seem inexpedient as well as unreasonable to you that the Judges should be expected to continue, for an indefinite period of time, under the present unsatisfactory relation existing between the different powers in the State ? The honest difficulties, which existed with me when I signed the letter addressed to your Honour on the 19th March, in conjunction with the other Judges, under the distinct understanding expressed therein, must continue to exist until the understanding shall have been performed. I may with all diffidence be allowed to observe that, in order to avert a crisis, I deemed it my duty to meet the Government and the Volksraad as far as I possibly could. I do not desire to go behind the understanding then arrived at.

Nothing will please me more than that this understanding shall, both in letter and in spirit, be faithfully carried out by both parties.

Trusting that this expression of my views may prove of service to your Honour,

I subscribe myself

Your obedient servant,

J. G. Kotzé,

Chief Justice.

No. 29.

Government Office, Pretoria, July 16, 1897.

The Honourable J. G. Kotzé,
Chief Justice, Pretoria.

YOUR HONOUR,

I am instructed to acknowledge the receipt of your letter of 8th inst., addressed by you as Chief Justice to His Honour the State President; and by way of reply to call your attention to the following :—

Permit me, however, first of all, in order to avoid a possible misunderstanding on your part, to point out that an omission occurs in your reference to the Executive Council Resolution, Art. 350 of 29th April last, which omission His Honour, of course, considers to be purely accidental. The insertion of the omitted words is nevertheless of some importance. According to your letter the words are—

"Resolves to advise His Honour the State President to propose to the Honourable the First Volksraad the appointment of a Commission of three or five members, whose duty it will be," etc., whereas the correct reading is, "Resolves to advise His Honour the State President to propose to the Honourable the First Volksraad the appointment of a Commission of three or five members, either from among its own number, or partly or entirely from outside its own number," etc.

Your assertion, which follows hereon, with reference to the letter of 19th March, by the Judges to the State President, that they have undertaken not to test laws and resolutions of the Volksraad by reference to the Grondwet under the understanding therein mentioned, is beyond doubt correct. His Honour the State President deems it, however, necessary to object to the assertion that a departure from this understanding has taken place, in the manner as set forth by your Honour. You say that "His Honour has not submitted any draft with the assistance of the Judges as aforesaid," to the Honourable the First Volksraad; that the Volksraad has been requested "to choose a commission in order to regulate several matters in connection with the Law No. 2 of 1896;" and that the entrusting to a Volksraad Commission of the task which His Honour had personally taken upon himself is no compliance with the understanding; "that His Honour the State President has undertaken to submit a draft to the Volksraad after having consulted the Judges;" that your Honour desires that the Judges "according to the understanding should be previously consulted, and that no mention is made as to time-limit in the authority given to the Commission of the First Volksraad, nor does any provision on the point occur in the proposal of the Government, notwithstanding the fact that His Honour has undertaken to submit the draft as speedily as possible."

With regard to these points His Honour the State President deems it necessary clearly to point out that he finds no mention of any understanding with regard to the assistance, advice, and consultation of the Judges, in the letter of the Judges, or in the answer thereto. In the letter of the Honourable the Judges the following passage merely occurs: "In the drawing up of such a draft the Judges are prepared to give the Government and the Volksraad every possible assistance." The answer to this portion of the letter of the Judges is to be found in the last part of the letter of the State Secretary, where he says, "His Honour also begs to thank the Judges for their statement that they are prepared to render the Government and Volksraad every possible assistance in connection therewith."

His Honour likewise considers it necessary to object to the very narrow, His Honour had almost said forced, construction given by you to the understanding, viz. that His Honour would submit a draft to the Volksraad. His Honour the State President trusts that your Honour, influenced by a reasonable construction of the understanding, will not conclude from his words "that what is said by the Judges with regard to the Grondwet agrees with his own intention," that His Honour has thereby precluded himself from having suggestions for the revision of the Grondwet drawn up by a commission appointed from among the members of the First Volksraad, or appointed partly or entirely from without such body, and acting in consultation with the Government. The clear intention of the understanding is this: that His Honour, the State President, promised his aid to obtain a Grondwet, guaranteeing, among other things, the independence of the High Court, which should be placed upon a stable basis, a promise which His Honour considers to have fulfilled. To obtain this end, as His Honour thinks you will admit, is not possible without the Volksraad, and it accordingly lay in the nature of the case first of all to ascertain from that Honourable Body whether it could agree to an amendment as desired by the State President and the Judges. The adoption of this course was the more necessary seeing that a Grondwet was definitely fixed last year, in which, as you will be aware, the Volksraad was not well disposed to adopt new principles. *Ex superabundanti* His Honour wishes to add that the necessity for the drawing up of the draft with the Volksraad was in March last recognized by the Judges themselves. Your Honour, in the letter of 19th March, indeed yourself clearly states that in the drawing up of such a draft the Judges are prepared not merely to give the Government but also the Volksraad every possible assistance.

This (now obtained) approval [of the Volksraad] must contribute to a more probable and speedy attainment of the object in view. That, with the view to the understanding to submit the matter as speedily as possible, no mention thereof is made in the proposal of the Government (resolution of the Executive Council), regard being had to the earnestness which His Honour has shown in laying it before the First Volksraad, and in such a manner that the advancement of the matter has been assured in the best possible way, is a circumstance which cannot be regarded as any material objection, and His Honour is convinced that you share his view, when he says that the obtaining of a revision of the Grondwet requires the necessary time, as definite proposals for the purpose can only be submitted to the Volksraad after due consideration. For the rest, His Honour agrees with you that a revision of the Grondwet in the desired direction will also necessitate certain alterations in the local laws; but it does not appear correct to His Honour to say that the definite proposal for such revision of the Grondwet will, as a necessary consequence of the resolution of the Executive, have to stand over until the codification of the laws shall have been completed.

Your Honour lays emphasis on the necessary amendment, by virtue of which any alteration of the Grondwet shall in future alone take place by means of special legislation. The Executive Council resolution already mentions the making of provision in the draft to the effect that no alterations of the Grondwet shall take place other than in the manner prescribed by the Grondwet itself, and in the drawing up of the draft it was and remains His Honour's intention to take the Orange Free State Constitution as an example in this respect.

With regard to your assertion that there is nothing to prevent the submission of the draft Grondwet, drawn up in January, 1894, once more to the Honourable the Volksraad, His Honour the State President wishes to observe that, as you will remember, the Volksraad has already expressed a clear opinion against such draft, and His Honour consequently thinks that it will not promote the speedy fulfilment so much desired by you for him to lay this draft once again before the Volksraad.

Your Honour states that you have, on this occasion, alone approached the State President, and do not know whether you are to presume that the other Judges, who together with you have signed the letter of 19th March, have departed from the position taken up by them therein.

When His Honour considers the serious meaning and gravity of the question, he cannot believe that they would depart from the position once taken up by them without having well-grounded and weighty reasons for so doing.

His Honour flatters himself with the thought that there exist with him no reasons which can lead to the conclusion that he was not or does not remain prepared most cordially to carry out what he intended when he sent his answer of the 22nd March last.

His Honour the State President thanks you for your expression of the desire that all possible difficulty may be prevented. He does not doubt that all misunderstanding, which even with the best intention is possible, and which His Honour thinks has also existed in this matter, will be removed by this his explanation of the subject.

In conclusion, His Honour wishes to inform you that he has every reason to think that possible alterations in the Grondwet, at any rate such as relate to the position of the High Court, will not be proposed to the Volksraad without the Judges having had an opportunity of giving their valued opinion thereon, not as a necessary consequence of the correspondence carried on in March last, but as a natural result of the respect felt for the High Court.

I have the honour to be
Your obedient servant,
C. VAN BAESCHOTEN,
Acting State Secretary.

No. 30.

Pretoria, 6.40 p.m., July 14, 1897.

From   To
  A. D. Wolmerans,   His Honour
     Chairman First Volksraad-   Chief Justice,
Commission for Revision of Grondwet.   Johannesburg.

A letter of the following tenor has been posted you this evening begins: On behalf of the Commission appointed by resolution of the Honourable the First Volksraad in the matter of the revision of the Grondwet, I have the honour to invite you, in the event of such being thought desirable by you and your colleagues, to nominate one or two of the Judges from your midst, in order to aid the Commission in drawing up a draft for the revision of the Grondwet (Law No. 2 of 1896). I have further the honour to request you to furnish me with an answer to this letter as speedily as possible, in order that the Commission may be enabled to complete the task entrusted to it with the desired speed ; ends,

(Signed) A. D. WOLMERANS,

Chairman.

W. J. GEERLING,

Secretary.

No. 31.

Johannesburg, July 14, 1897.

From   To A. D. Wolmerans,

Chief Justice.   Chairman of the Volksraad-

Commission, Pretoria.

Your telegram received. Am at present engaged here in Circuit Court. Will return Saturday, and immediately summon my colleagues on subject of your telegram, and communicate again with you later on.

No. 32.

Circuit Court, S.A. Republic, Johannesburg, 16, 7, 1897.

A. D. Wolmerans, Esq.,

Chairman of the Commission

of the First Volksraad for

Revision of the Grondwet.

Sir,

I am instructed by His Honour the Chief Justice to acknowledge the receipt of your letter, dated 14th July, 1897, and to inform you that His Honour has received a telegram from you of the same nature to which he telegraphed you the following reply: "Your telegram received. Am at present engaged here in Circuit Court. Will return Saturday, and immediately summon my colleagues on subject of your telegram, and communicate again with you later on."

I am now instructed to confirm this telegram by way of answer to your letter.

I have the honour to be

Your obedient servant,

W. J. SCHOLTZ,

Assistant Registrar.

No. 33.

Pretoria, July 19, 1897.

A. D. Wolmerans, Esq.,
Chairman of the First
Volksraad-Commission for
Revision of the Grondwet.

SIR,

I have the honour to inform you that all the Judges could unfortunately not meet together yesterday. I have accordingly, in consequence of your letter and telegram of 14th inst., approached each of my colleagues in writing. As soon as I receive their answers I will again communicate with you. I leave to-day for Johannesburg, in order to continue the sitting of the Circuit Court at that place.

I have the honour to be

Your obedient servant,

J. G. KOTZÉ,

Chief Justice.

No. 34.

High Court, Pretoria, July 19, 1897.

The Honourable
Mr. Justice Ameshoff.

Your Honour,
I am instructed by the Honourable the Chief
Justice to request you, in consequence of a certain telegram
and letter of Mr. A. D. Wolmerans, Chairman of the First
Volksraad-Commission for revision of the Grondwet, and dated
14th July, to furnish His Honour the Chief Justice at your
earliest convenience with your views on the subject of the
request contained in said letter and telegram, in order that
His Honour may be able to send Mr. Wolmerans a definite
reply. The Chief Justice returns to Johannesburg this day to
continue the Circuit Court there, and will probably not return
until Friday or Saturday. He therefore desires that your
Honour will kindly forward your answer to him at Johannesburg.
I have the honour to be
Your Honour's obedient servant,
L. F. B. JUTA,
Assistant Registrar.
P.S.—Copy of telegram and letter, which are of even tenor,
goes herewith.

No. 35.

Pretoria, July 19, 1897.

From   To Chief Justice,
Judge Gregorowski.   Circuit Court,
                                                Johannesburg.

With reference to the letter received from your secretary,
I think immediate compliance should be given to the letter of

the Chairman of the Commission in connection with the Grondwet, and two judges ought to be nominated to assist the Commission.

No. 36.

High Court, S.A.R., Pretoria, July 20, 1897.

The Honourable
The Chief Justice.

YOUR HONOUR,

In answer to your letter of 19th July, I wish to inform you that I think the only chance of obtaining a proper Grondwet is to appoint two judges in order to aid the Commission, as proposed in the letter of Mr. A. D. Wolmerans.

Your obedient servant,

GEORGE T. MORICE.

No. 37.

Pretoria, July 20, 1897.

The Honourable
The Chief Justice.

In answer to a communication addressed to me yesterday on your behalf by the Registrar, with regard to a certain letter and telegram of Mr. A. D. Wolmerans', Chairman of the Grondwet Revision Commission, I have the honour to state, as my opinion on the subject, that I deem it my duty to meet the wishes of the Commission whenever it so desires, and I therefore declare myself prepared to assist the Commission in its labours should your Honour nominate me for the purpose.

I have the honour to be

Your obedient servant,

J. ESSER,

Judge.

No. 38.

High Courts, S.A.R., Pretoria, July 22, 1897.

The Honourable J. G. Kotzé,
    Chief Justice.

YOUR HONOUR,

With regard to the invitation of the Volksraad Commission for the revision of the Grondwet, etc., communicated to me in writing by you, and whereby the Court is requested to nominate one or two of its members to work with the Volksraad-Commission, I have the honour to answer that I would very much like to co-operate in order to obtain as good a revision of the Grondwet as possible, but that with that view I do not deem it desirable that I should personally attend the sittings of the Commission. The duties connected with my office, the necessity to hold Circuit Court sittings, will prevent me from regularly attending the Commission.

My assistance will be much more effectual when I shall be in a position to advise upon the draft as a whole, in order to inform the people of the Republic of the necessity and desirability of the proposed alterations, or the alterations which may yet be added.

It is my desire that your Honour will acquaint the Volksraad-Commission with this my letter.

I have the honour to be
            Your obedient servant,
                    E. J. P. JORISSEN.

No. 39.

High Court of the S.A.R., Pretoria, July 22, 1897.

The Honourable
    The Chief Justice,
        Pretoria.

YOUR HONOUR,

In answer to your communication of 19th July, I have the honour to acquaint you hereby with my views regarding the request contained in the telegram of Mr. A. D. Wolmerans, Chairman of the Honourable the First Volksraad-Commission for revision of the Grondwet.

It will be necessary to go back to the letter of 19th March, also signed by myself. In this letter the Judges offer their assistance in revising the Grondwet. I state here at once in writing that I personally have understood therefrom that whenever the opinion of the Judges should be desired, such would take place in a manner in the fixing of which the Judges would have been consulted. The measure which has now been resolved upon has, however, been taken without their co-operation. I acknowledge without any reservation the right of the Government to act thus. I do not agree with your view that the offer of assistance by the Judges in their letter of 19th March, and the acceptance thereof by the State President, place His Honour under the obligation, or compel him, to call in such assistance. As a measure has now been adopted which has resulted in the existence of a Volksraad-Commission, I should like to point to the practice formerly observed in a similar instance by Volksraad and Court. I refer to the Grondwet-Commission, of which Mr. TalJaard was Chairman in 1887 or 1888. On that occasion the written opinion of all the Judges was asked and given, and these were published in the *Gazette* and laid before the people. Every one could therefore judge for himself of what was thus made public.

The request now addressed to you places us on another standpoint. I quite agree with the views expounded by His Honour the State President in the First Volksraad, that it is desirable that the Volksraad shall co-operate, whether it be by way of Commission, in the preparation of proposals for such an important matter as the revision of the Grondwet, but I also agree with those members of the Honourable the Volksraad who have opposed the proposed measure as being unconstitutional. The proper course, which in my opinion ought to have been followed, is a middle one.

Had I been consulted, I would probably have suggested that the Government should draw up and propose a draft declaring the necessity for a revision, and regulating the manner in which this was to take place, and that then the Volksraad, availing itself of Article 12 of the Grondwet, 1896, should immediately take such draft-law into consideration, and declare further that this draft should be published for three months, and after such publication to consider and pass it in a session specially convened for the purpose.

This law might have provided that, without binding the Government thereto in this difficult question, a Commission of advice should be added to it; the law might have provided who should be a member of such Commission by choice from among, or outside of, the Volksraad, or by indicating who should *ex officio* take part in the deliberations; further how this Commission should assemble, and whether its sittings should be public and the minutes published in the *Gazette* for the information and guidance of the burghers, etc., etc.

In this way the reasonable desire of His Honour the State President, and likewise the just objections of the members who were in opposition, would have been met, and I may add my own objections also, which occurred to me by reason of the request that has been made. I must honestly acknowledge that I do not precisely know where I am.

Nevertheless it is desired that two Judges shall aid the Commission. What is the position of these Judges? Are they members having a vote, or merely advisory members? In the former case they will have the right to inquire into the legality of their existence. If such should be my duty, then the conclusion to which I would come will, regard being had to what I have already remarked, be clear to every one. Should I be an advising member, then I can, as an honourable man, give the Commission no other advice than that it owes it as a duty to itself to commence by placing itself in a lawful position. It might be contended that the Government remains free to adopt the report of the Commission as its own, and to submit it to the First Volksraad. This would be the case were it not that the Commission is and remains a Volksraad-Commission, and is therefore obliged to report to the Volksraad. The Government has therefore disappeared from the whole transaction.

I now find myself placed face to face with a great difficulty.

Where I would so much have liked to have given my assistance, I believe that I can for the present do nothing else but content myself with the polite intimation of my difficulties, and thankfully acknowledge the good intentions which actuate the Commission.

I also deem it my duty to inform you that I will decline voluntarily to sit on any Commission for the purpose of revising the Grondwet, if there be present on such Commission men who, by their legal advice, have directly or indirectly co-operated to bring about the passing of the so-called Law No. 1, 1897. I do not consider it necessary to give my reasons for this. Should a law as indicated by me place me under the obligation of taking part in the meetings, I will obey it.

I have the honour to be

Your obedient servant,

H. A. AMESHOFF,

1st Puisne Judge.

No. 40.

Pretoria, July 27, 1897.

A. D. Wolmerans, Esq.,
　　Chairman of the Commission
　　　　of the First Volksraad
　　　　　　for Revision of the Grondwet.

SIR,

With regard to my letter of 19th July addressed to you, I have now the honour to enclose herewith for your information the answers which I have received from my colleagues to my communication to them in consequence of your telegram and letter of 14th July. From these it will be clear to the Commission of the Honourable the First Volksraad for the revision of the Grondwet what the opinion of each of my colleagues is on the subject. In consequence of these answers I find it difficult to nominate one or two Judges to aid your Commission. As, however, Judges Morice, Gregorowski, and Esser are prepared, without more, to assist your Commission in carrying out your important duty, an opportunity is afforded your Honourable Commission to call in one or two of these Judges for the purpose of aiding your Commission as it may deem fit.

I desire to avail myself of this opportunity to assure your Commission, and through it the Honourable the First Volksraad, that I am prepared to give your Commission, as originally appointed by the Volksraad, every assistance, whenever my advice on any point may be required, but I can only do so in writing, and this for the following reasons :—

I place myself entirely on the standpoint taken up by me in the letter of the Judges to the State President, dated the 19th March, and which was acquiesced in without any qualification by the President in his answer of the 22nd March. An understanding of a solemn nature was thereby entered into before the people and the civilized world. In the spirit of this understanding I offer my assistance.

I am also informed that your Commission has nominated as advising members certain gentlemen, who in my opinion are directly and indirectly responsible for the measure known as Law No. 1 of 1897. Regard being had to the nature of this measure, it has become impossible for me to be present, and work together with these learned gentlemen. I do not wish to enlarge upon this point at present. As an honourable man you will easily appreciate the objection of another honourable man.

I entertain the hope that the much desired and necessary new Grondwet will put an end to all possible misunderstanding, and that by means of a thoroughly effectual constitution, rendering to each of the powers in the State its just due, the country and its people may look forward to a continued period of rest and prosperity.

I have the honour to be
Your obedient servant,
J. G. KOTZÉ,
Chief Justice.

No. 41.

Pretoria, July 30, 1897.

The Honourable J. G. Kotzé,
    Chief Justice of the S.A.R., Pretoria.

Your Honour,
        I have the honour to acknowledge the receipt of your communication of 27th inst., enclosing letters from the different members of the High Court, addressed to you in consequence of my telegram and letter of 14th July to your Honour in the matter of the invitation to the High Court on behalf of the Commission of the Honourable the First Volksraad *re* revision of the Grondwet, for you to nominate one or two members for the purpose of aiding the said Commission in carrying out its labours.

These letters have been submitted by me to the Commission, which has duly noted the contents, and the Commission regrets that your Honour could not see your way to complying with its request.

I have the honour to be
        Your Honour's obedient servant,
                A. D. WOLMERANS,
                        Chairman of the Commission.
                W. J. GEERLING,
                        Secretary.

No. 42.

Pretoria, S.A. Republic, September 10, 1897.

His Honour
    The State President.

Your Honour,
        I have the honour to acknowledge the receipt of a letter dated 16th July, 1897, and addressed to me by the Acting State Secretary, containing the answer of your Honour to my communication of 8th July. I have no wish to create a correspondence, and consequently I will make but one remark.

After duly considering your answer, I regret that I cannot see my way to sharing your views. I approached you simply for the purpose of preventing misunderstanding and difficulty. The obtaining a Grondwet, safeguarded against sudden changes, and providing for the pure, dignified, and independent administration of justice, as set forth in the understanding, is my only object, as it ought also to be the object of every burgher and friend of the country. What effect the opposite of this, viz. a Grondwet exposed to sudden and hasty alterations, and a dependent and subordinate judicature, will have on the credit and progress of the Republic is a question which I, as Judge, do not at present wish to consider. I merely desire that the High Court shall continue independent and inviolate in the exercise of its functions.

With respect, I have the honour to be

Your Honour's obedient servant,

J. G. KOTZÉ,

Chief Justice.

No. 43.

Pretoria, November 12, 1897.

His Honour

The Chief Justice of the S.A. Republic,

Pretoria.

YOUR HONOUR,

With regard to your letter of 27th July last, addressed to my Commission *re* revision of the Grondwet, and from which the Commission understands that your Honour is disposed to give written advice in this important matter, I have the honour, on behalf of my Commission, to ask you whether you and your colleagues, who do not already act in conjunction with my Commission, wish to make any proposals with respect to that portion of the Grondwet which relates to the Judicial Power.

The labours of my Commission have, to its regret, been delayed, seeing that the consideration of the "Industrial Report" had to take precedence. The Commission, however, hopes in the mean time to resume its labours during the special session of the Honourable the First Volksraad in February, 1898, and will then value the receipt of any proposals as indicated above from your Honour.

I have the honour to be

Your obedient servant,

A. D. WOLMERANS,

Chairman of the First Volksraad-Commission for

Revision of the Grondwet.

W. J. GEERLING,

Secretary.

No. 44.

High Court, Pretoria, December 15, 1897.

His Honour

S. J. P. Kruger,

State President.

YOUR HONOUR,

Regard being had to the agreement arrived at between you, as Head of the State, and the Judges, in March last, and to my letters of July 8 and September 10, 1897, addressed to your Honour, I now have the honour to call your attention to the fact that the session of the Honourable the First Volksraad has come to a close without, in terms of the said understanding, any draft measure having been submitted to the First Volksraad for its preliminary approval, pending the further confirmation thereof by the people. I will be much obliged to your Honour to be informed of the reasons for departing from the understanding concerning a draft Grondwet, and what your Honour now proposes to do in order to return to the course originally indicated.

With respect, I subscribe myself

Your Honour's obediently,

J. G. KOTZE,

Chief Justice.

No. 45.

High Court of the S.A. Republic, Pretoria, February 5, 1898.

His Honour
     S. J. P. Kruger,
       State President.

YOUR HONOUR,

I regret that circumstances compel me to write you this letter. I do so in continuance of my previous communications of 8th July and 15th December, 1897, addressed to you. I have been anxious not to act with any precipitation, and have waited until the time fixed for the election of President has passed, in order that the importance and significance of the untenable position existing between the various powers in the State may be calmly considered.

According to the understanding arrived at in March last between the State President and the Judges, the latter undertook not to test laws and resolutions of the Honourable the Volksraad by reference to the Grondwet, pending the laying before the First Volksraad by your Honour of a draft Grondwet, providing

       (*a*) That the Constitution shall alone be altered in a special way, after the example contained on the subject in the Orange Free State Constitution; and

       (*b*) That the guarantees for the independence of the Judiciary should be incorporated in such Constitution.

In March, 1897, your Honour undertook to submit this draft Grondwet as speedily as possible to the Honourable the First

Volksraad. I have already, in my letter of the 8th July last, observed that the understanding has been departed from by your Honour, and especially in two respects, viz. 1st, with regard to the course of procedure adopted by you ; and 2nd, with regard to the limitation of time. In my letter of 8th July I dwelt upon the desirability and necessity of returning to the course indicated by the understanding. I also pointed out that the Judges cannot for an indefinite period of time continue under the present unsatisfactory and uncertain relation existing between the various powers in the State. Permit me once more to remind your Honour of the fact that, in order to avoid a collision and a crisis, which would have shaken the credit and the existence of the Republic as a constitutionally governed country to their deepest foundations, the Judges deemed it their duty, as far as they possibly could, to meet the Volksraad and the Executive by signing the written understanding. I referred to this point in my previous letter, and declared that nothing would be more pleasing to me than that this understanding should be loyally carried out by both sides. To my regret I find that the action of the Judges has not been appreciated. Although I have patiently awaited the performance of the understanding, no draft Grondwet has, in terms of the understanding, been laid by your Honour before the Honourable the First Volksraad during its session from 3rd May until 17th November, 1897, nor have any steps been taken for removing the measure which bears the name of Law No. 1, 1897. As long as this does not take place, the existing legal uncertainty remains, and the violation of the independence of the Judiciary continues.

I do not seek to magnify my office, yet it is my duty to see that the complete independence of the Judiciary, as guaranteed by law, and the protection of the Judges in the exercise of their judicial functions entrusted to them by the people in the Constitution, shall remain entirely free and inviolate. To have ensured this and the carrying out of the understanding by your Honour entailed neither time nor trouble. A draft could have been drawn up in a comparatively short time, for all that was necessary for a compliance with the terms of the understanding consists in the addition of one article to the Grondwet, whereby the Constitution would be guarded against sudden changes, and the Judiciary protected. A simple draft article of, for instance, the following or similar tenor would have sufficed :—

"The Grondwet cannot be altered, except the proposal for the purpose be on each occasion first published three months previously, and adopted in two consecutive ordinary annual sessions of the First Volksraad."

If, then, the already existing guarantees for the independence of the Judiciary (which have been violated by the measure known as Law No. 1, 1897) be incorporated in the Grondwet with a simple addition in regard to the fixing of the Judges' salaries, as contained in the North American Constitution, and recently also proposed in the Orange Free State, everything would have been already on the right road for the consideration and approval of the Volksraad and people, and the understanding would have been loyally carried out. A whole year has now been lost.

If in March last I considered it my duty to sign the understanding, and, depending upon the speedy performance thereof by your Honour, to regard myself as bound thereby, I now equally deem it my duty to observe and declare that the understanding is of a reciprocal nature. If it be not observed, or be departed from, by the one party, it is no longer binding on the other party, and such is unfortunately the position at which we have arrived. The only protection which I, as Judge, possess, and the only honourable and constitutional course which I can adopt, is to intimate to your Honour that I consider the understanding of March, 1897, as having lapsed and no longer existing.

With respect, I subscribe myself

Your Honour's obediently,

J. G. KOTZÉ,

Chief Justice.

No. 46.

Pretoria, February 7, 1898.

A. D. Wolmerans, Esq.,
Chairman of the First
Volksraad-Commission,
re Revision of the Grondwet.

SIR,

Now that I have returned from my vacation, I have much pleasure in sending your Commission the following answer to your letter of 12th November, 1897, more especially as you have informed me that your Commission hopes to resume its labours during the approaching February session of the Honourable the First Volksraad, which commences on the 14th inst.

So far as I understand them, my colleagues, Judges Ameshoff and Jorissen, do not at present see their way clear to express any opinion with regard to the nature of a revision of the Grondwet. Since my letter to you, of 27th July, the position, so far as the understanding arrived at between the State President and the Judges in March last is concerned, has in my opinion altered. I am, however, always prepared, wherever I can do so, to give a Volksraad-Commission the benefit of my advice.

In the Law No. 2 of 1896 several guarantees for the independence of the Judiciary are to be found. (*Vide* Artt. 15; 82; 86; 139, of Law No. 2, 1896). To these existing guarantees a few further provisions should be added, *e.g.* a provision with reference to the fixing of the salaries of the Judges, such as has recently been proposed in the Orange Free State, and already exists in the Constitution of the United States of North America; and a provision that the Grondwet or Constitution can alone be altered by means of special legislation in the following or some similar manner: *e.g.* "The Grondwet can alone be altered where a proposal to that effect has been published three months beforehand, and has been adopted in two successive ordinary

D

sessions of the First Volksraad." If a certain stipulated majority of votes is desired for the purpose, as provided in the Constitution of the sister Republic, there is nothing to prevent the insertion of such a clause.

These guarantees are necessary for the independence of the Judiciary. In the hope that these suggestions may prove of some service to your Commission,

I have the honour to be

Your obedient servant,

J. G. Kotzé,

Chief Justice.

No. 47.

Government Office, Pretoria, February 16, 1898.

His Honour
>   J. G. Kotzé,
>   Chief Justice,
>   Pretoria.

Your Honour,

I have the honour to acknowledge the receipt of your letter, dated 5th February last, in which you state that you consider your declaration of the 19th March, 1897, that you, especially also after the decided expression of opinion of the Honourable the First Volksraad on this point, would not test the existing and future laws and Volksraad resolutions by reference to the Grondwet, as having lapsed and no longer existing.

This, your declaration of 19th March, 1897, cannot and may not be considered as a contract. No agreement can be entered into by a Judge with regard to the laws which he shall or shall not apply. The declaration required by the law must be absolute, and cannot be subjected to conditions.

Seeing that your answer to the letter of the State Secretary, dated 4th March, 1897, wherein, on my behalf, the question mentioned in Article 4 of Law No. 1 of 1897 has been put, is now declared by yourself as no longer existing, I must consider that you wish it to be understood that there is no answer from you.

Seeing that Article 4 of Law No. 1 of 1897 empowers me to dismiss those members of the High Court from whom I receive either a negative, or, in my opinion, unsatisfactory reply, or no reply within the stipulated time, and seeing that your answer must now be considered by me as not existing, or if existing, as insufficient, I am, to my deep regret, obliged to proceed to the last step with regard to yourself, and you are hereby, in terms of Article 4 of Law No. 1 of 1897, dismissed from your office as Chief Justice of the S.A. Republic, to take effect from this date.

I have the honour to be

Your obedient servant,

S. J. P. KRUGER,

State President.

No. 48.

High Court, Pretoria, February 16, 1898.

His Honour
    S. J. P. Kruger,
        State President.

YOUR HONOUR,

I have the honour to acknowledge the receipt of your letter of to-day's date in answer to mine of 5th inst., in which you inform me at the end thereof that you have deemed it fit to dismiss me forthwith from my office of Chief Justice of the S.A. Republic.

Your Honour must not take it amiss when I point out to

you the untenableness and illegality of your action. You say
that my "declaration of 19th March, 1897 (*i.e.* the declaration
of the five Judges), cannot and may not be considered as being
a contract. No agreement can be entered into by a Judge with
regard to the laws which he will or will not apply. The
declaration must, according to the law, be absolute, and cannot
be subject to conditions." When you, as State President,
entered into the understanding, in March last, with the Judges,
you were of an entirely different opinion, and considered that
the circumstances did indeed justify the acceptance by you of
the understanding proposed by the Judges. Permit me to
remind your Honour of the understanding.

"The Judges declare this upon the understanding that your
Honour will as speedily as possible submit a draft to the
honourable the Volksraad, whereby the constitution or Grondwet (guaranteeing, *inter alia,* the independence of the High
Court) will be placed on a sure basis," etc. This understanding
proposed by the Judges you unreservedly accepted. You were,
therefore, as State President, a party to the understanding,
which was as binding upon you as upon the Judges. The
obligation thereby created was unquestionably of a reciprocal
nature, and subjected both sides to the terms of a solemn
compact.

The measure, under which your Honour affects to act, does
not in Article 4 confer the competence on the State President
of repeatedly putting the intended question to the members of
the Judiciary. He can only do so once. To the question put
to me, together with the other Judges, in March last, an answer
has, in terms of the understanding, already been given and
accepted. Moreover, I cannot admit the legality of the
measure, which bears the name of Law No. 1, 1897. My
appointment as Judge is for life; in the independent discharge
of my judicial functions I may not be interfered with; and
where I have been guilty of any supposed judicial misdemeanour
I must be properly indicted, and can only be found guilty and
punished by a specially constituted tribunal.

These guarantees have been established, not only for the
protection of the Judges, but also for that of the people, and of

all the inhabitants in the State. These guarantees have been introduced, and are assured by Law No. 2 of 1896, and prior laws, by the convention with England and the Grondwet of 1858. The measure, therefore, which bears the name of Law No. 1 of 1897, which, I may add, was never previously published for the information of the people, and was, in the short space of three days, accepted by the Honourable the Volksraad upon your Honour's urgent request, possesses (I say it with all deference) no legal validity. By assuming and carrying out an authority that is illegal; by violating the guarantees for the independence of the Judiciary, the condition under which the Republic exists as a civilized and constitutionally governed country is likewise broken.

I regret, therefore, that for these reasons I cannot agree with your Honour's views, nor can I admit the legality of your action. Until I am properly and legally found guilty by a competent Court and dismissed from office, I am, and remain, Chief Justice.

I have the honour to be

Your Honour's obedient servant,

J. G. KOTZÉ,

.   Chief Justice.

No. 49.

Government Office, Pretoria, February 17, 1898.

J. G. Kotzé, Esq.,

Pretoria.

SIR,

In reply to your letter to His Honour the State President, dated High Court of the South African Republic, Pretoria, February 16, 1898, and signed by you with the addition of the title of Chief Justice, I have the honour to inform

you, on the instruction of His Honour, that His Honour abides
by his decision, and considers the matter as ended thereby.

I have the honour to be

Your obedient servant,

Dr. W. J. Leyds,

State Secretary.

No. 50.

Resolved: That this meeting of Members of the Bar and
Side Bar in Johannesburg (a) Expresses its regret that the
Executive of this State should have exercised the powers claimed
under the Measure known as Law No. 1 of 1897, by adopting its
recent action towards Chief Justice Kotzé; (b) considers that
any undue interference by the Executive with the Judiciary is
contrary to the best interests of the State; (c) considers that the
action adopted against Chief Justice Kotzé is calculated to bring
discredit on this State and its legal system, and is unconstitutional and illegal; (d) considers that it will be derogatory to the
honour and dignity of the profession if any of its Members
accept the Judicial Office subject to the Measure known as Law
No. 1 of 1897.

Resolved: That this meeting of Members of the Bar and
Side Bar in Johannesburg expresses its sympathy with and
confidence in Chief Justice Kotzé and approval of the attitude
which he has adopted in the present Judicial crisis, in which
they will support him to the best of their ability.

Resolved: That having regard to the Resolution passed at a
meeting similar to this on the 25th February, 1897, this meeting
re-affirms the principle of such Resolution which reads as
follows:—

"That the principle of the Bill is not only bad, but distinctly
dangerous, inasmuch as it seeks to deprive the Judiciary of
that independence which is the chief safeguard of the people's
rights and liberties."

Although the principle of this resolution is not affected by the agreement come to between the Government and the Judges in March, 1897, yet this meeting regrets and views with concern the practical repudiation of that agreement by the Government.

Resolved : That copies of these resolutions be forwarded to the Executive Council, Chief Justice Kotzé, and the Incorporated Law Society without delay.

APPENDIX.

A.

His Honour
  The State President.

YOUR HONOUR,

In answer to the letters addressed to the Judges, whereby they are asked whether they deem it in accordance with their oath and duty to administer justice according to the existing and future laws and Volksraad resolutions, and not to arrogate to themselves any so-called testing right, the Judges have the honour to inform your Honour that they do not feel themselves at liberty to give any answer.

Should your Honour desire to know why the Judges are of opinion that they are not at liberty to give any answer, they are prepared to give you their reasons for this opinion.

The Judges have the honour to subscribe themselves

Your obedient servants,

J. G. KOTZÉ.
H. A. AMESHOFF.
E. J. P. JORISSEN.
GEORGE T. MORICE.
R. GREGOROWSKI.

[NOTE.—This answer, but for the arrival of Sir Henry de Villiers at Pretoria, and the subsequent written understanding entered into between the Judges and the President, would have been sent in to the latter by the former.—J. G. K.]

B.

From the letter of the undersigned to His Honour the State President, dated 19th March last, and the written answer of His Honour thereto, dated 22nd March, 1897, it appears that the Judges have undertaken not to test laws and resolutions of the Volksraad by reference to the Grondwet under the express understanding that His Honour would as speedily as possible submit to the Honourable Volksraad a *draft* by which the Constitution or Grondwet (guaranteeing *inter alia* the independence of the High Court) shall be placed on a stable basis, so that no alterations can be made therein save by special legislation, after the example of the provisions contained on the subject in the Constitution of the Orange Free State. The Judges at the same time offered their services to be of assistance in the drawing up of such a draft. All this was unreservedly accepted by His Honour, who expressed his pleasure to find that what was said by the Judges with regard to the Grondwet agreed with his plans and intentions.

The Judges feel themselves compelled to point out to His Honour that, according to their diffident opinion, this understanding has been departed from. They consider that such departure has taken place in the following respects, viz. :—

1st. No draft has been submitted by the State President to the Volksraad. Instead of such a draft being drawn up by the Government and the aid of the Judges, as they had a right to expect, from the letter of His Honour, called in, the responsibility of drawing up the draft has been transferred to a commission of the Honourable the Volksraad.

2nd. According to the understanding, the draft had to be submitted to the Volksraad as speedily as possible, and the undersigned Judges are of opinion that the course adopted by His Honour serves to defeat the understanding in this respect. Under Clause c of the proposal of the Government, and accepted by the Volksraad, it is resolved that the existing local laws shall be collected into a system as a whole. However desirable it may be to collect the existing legislation of the country into one systematic whole, this is not a matter referred to in the understanding between His Honour and the Judges. The objection of the Judges is that the systematic arrangement of all the laws of the South African Republic, together with the necessary amendment, alteration, and simplification thereof wherever necessary, is a gigantic task, which will take at least two or three years, and probably longer, for its completion. The carrying out of the understanding as appearing in the letters of 19th and 22nd March last is therefore indefinitely postponed, and the present unsatisfactory relation between the different powers in the State will in the mean time continue.

The undersigned make this communication to His Honour in no hostile spirit, but in the hope that His Honour will devise means to remove their objections and restore the desired co-operation between the different powers in the State.

[The above is the draft of a letter drawn up by Mr. Justice Morice in June, 1887, and which it was intended should be sent by all the five Judges to President Kruger.—J. G. K.]

C.

And yet a way out of the difficulty is possible, which will meet our objections, and render it easy for the State President to carry out the agreement in the sense which the Judges attach to it. We respectfully request your Honour to consider the suggestions we are about to make as the commencement of our promise to aid you with advice. First of all we would strongly urge that the collecting and systematizing of the existing laws should be kept entirely separate from the revising of the Grondwet, and this for the following two reasons: (1) This collecting, etc., cannot take place until the Grondwet has been established; and (2) when once the new Grondwet exists it will take even experts two or three years to complete such collection.

In the second place, we wish to remind your Honour that there exists a very good draft of a new Grondwet. In 1893 you appointed a Commission of experts to draw it up. In January, 1894, this draft was submitted for your approval and that of the Executive Council. You approved it, and published it in the *Gazette* for the information of the people.

We advise you to again publish this draft and lay it before the people, naturally with such alterations and additions as you may think expedient, after having consulted us Judges, who now again, even as in March last, tender their assistance. *This can be done within a couple of weeks; and when duly laid before the people the Volksraad can then, for instance in a special session in November next, create it into law.*

In this way an end will be put *within a few months* to all existing or supposed difficulties.

It goes without saying that the draft Grondwet of 1894 is not considered by us as being perfect, and incapable of improvement.

Additions to it may be necessary, especially with regard to the wishes and requirements of the new population that has come in. At any rate, it is a very good guide, and the majority of its *hundred* articles will have to be taken over in a new Grondwet. Alterations and perhaps additions may be necessary.

[This is an amended draft drawn up by Mr. Justice Jorissen, and which he considered should have been tacked on to the original draft of the letter by the Chief Justice. After several consultations between the five Judges, the four puisne Judges were not disposed to take any action. The Chief Justice thereupon alone wrote to the President on July 8, 1897. See No. 28.—J. G. K.]

LONDON :
PRINTED BY WILLIAM CLOWES AND SONS, LIMITED,
STAMFORD STREET AND CHARING CROSS.

www.ingramcontent.com/pod-product-compliance
Lightning Source LLC
Chambersburg PA
CBHW022154020726
47496CB00008B/2707